# The Parish Magazine, and The Love Affair of George Vincent Parker

Sir Arthur Conan Doyle

# THE PARISH MAGAZINE

By

Arthur Conan Doyle

1930

## THE PARISH MAGAZINE

It was six o'clock on a winter evening. Mr. Pomeroy, the printer, was on the point of leaving his office, which was his back room, for his home, which was his front room, when young Murphy entered. Murphy was an imperturbable youth with a fat face and sleepy eyes, who had the rare quality of always doing without question whatever he was told. It is usually a great virtue—but there are exceptions.

"There are two folk to see you," said Murphy, laying two cards upon the table.

Mr. Pomeroy glanced at them.

"Mr. Robert Anderson. Miss Julia Duncan. I don't know the names. Well, show them in."

A long, sad-faced youth entered, accompanied by a mournful young lady, clad in black. Their appearance was respectable, but depressing.

"I dare say you know this," said the youth, holding up a small, grey-covered volume, the outer cover of which was ornamented with the picture of a church. "It's the *St. Olivia's Church Magazine*. What I mean, it's the Parish Magazine. This lady and I are what you might call the editors. It has been printed by— —"

"Elliot and Dark, in the City," said the lady, as her companion seemed to stumble. "But they have suddenly closed down their works. We have the month's issue all ready, but we want to add to it."

"A Supplement, if you get my meaning," said the youth. "That's the word—supplement. The thing has become too dam' ——"

"What he is trying to say," cried the girl, "is that the magazine wants lighting up on the social side."

"That's it," said the youth. "Just a bit of ginger, so to speak. So we arranged a Supplement. We will put it in as a loose leaf, if you follow my meaning. It's all typewritten and clear"—here he drew a folded paper from his pocket—"and it needs no reading or correcting. Just rush it through, five hundred copies, as quickly as you can do it."

"The issue is overdue," said the lady. "We must have it out by midday to-morrow. They tell me Ferguson and Co. could easily have it ready in the time, and if you won't guarantee it, we must take it to them."

"Absolutely," said the youth.

Mr. Pomeroy picked up the typed copy and glanced at it. His eyes fell upon the words, "Our beloved Vicar, Mr. Ffolliott-Sharp, B.A." There was some allusion to a bishopric. Pomeroy threw the paper across to his assistant. "Get on with it!" he said.

"We should like to pay at once," said Miss Duncan, opening her bag. "Here is a five-pound note, and you can account for it afterwards. Of course, you don't know us, and might not trust us."

"Well, if one did not trust the Parish Magazine—" said Pomeroy, smiling.

"Absolutely," cried the youth. "But what I mean is that we want to pay now. You'll send the stuff round to me at 16 Colgrove Road. Got it? Not later than twelve. Rush it through. What?"

"It shall be there," said Pomeroy.

The pair were leaving the room when the girl turned back.

"Put your name as printer at the bottom," she said. "It's the law. Besides, you may get the printing of the Magazine in the future."

"Certainly. We always print our name."

The couple passed out, and hugged each other in the passage.

"I think we put it across," said he.

"Marvellous!" said she.

"That fiver was my idea."

"Incredible!" she cried. "We've got him."

"Absolutely!" said he, and they passed out into the night.

The stolid Murphy wrought long and hard, and the Pomeroy Press was working till unconscionable hours. The assistant found the matter less dull than most which he handled, and a smile spread itself occasionally over his fat face. Surely some of this was rather unusual stuff. He had never read anything quite like it. However, "his not to reason why". He had been well drilled to do exactly what he was told. The packet was ready next morning, and before twelve o'clock it had been duly dispatched to the house mentioned. Murphy carried it himself and was surprised to find their client waiting for it at the garden gate. It took some energy, apparently, to be the editor of a Parish Magazine.

It was twenty-four hours before the bomb burst, which blew Mr. Pomeroy and his household into fragments. The first intimation of trouble was the following letter:

*"Sir,*

*"We can hardly Imagine that you have read the contents of the so-called Supplement to the Parish Magazine which has been distributed to the members of the congregation of St. Olivia's Church. If you had you would hardly have dared to make yourself responsible by putting your name to it. I need not say that you are likely to hear a good deal more of the matter. As to my teeth, I may say that they are remarkably sound, and that I have never been to a dentist in my life.*

*"James Wilson*

*"(Major)."*

There was a second letter upon the breakfast table. The dazed printer picked it up. It was in a feminine hand, and read thus:

"*Sir,*

"*With regard to the infamous paragraph in the new issue of the Parish Magazine, I may say that if I have bought a new car it is no business of anyone else, and the remarks about my private affairs are most unkind and uncalled for. I understand that as you are the printer you are legally responsible. You will hear in the course of a few days from my legal advisers.*

"*Yours faithfully,*

"Jane Peddigrew.

"14, *Elton Square.*"

"What the devil does it mean?" cried Pomeroy, staring wildly at his wife and daughter. "Murphy! Murphy!"

His assistant entered from the office.

"Have you a copy of that Supplement, which you printed for the Parish Magazine?"

"Yes, sir. I delivered five hundred, but there are a few in the office."

"Bring it in! Bring it in! Quick!"

Then Mr. Pomeroy began to read aloud, and apoplexy grew nearer and nearer. The document was headed Social Notes, and began with several dates and allusions to services which might give confidence to the superficial and rapid reader. Then it opened out in this way:

"'Our beloved Vicar (Mr. Ffolliott-Sharp, B.A.) is still busy trying to wangle a bishopric. This time he says in his breezy way that it is 'a perfect sitter', but we have our doubts. It is notorious that he has pulled strings in the past, and that the said strings broke. However, he has a cousin in the Lord Chancellor's office, so there is always hope.'

"Gracious!" cried Pomeroy. "In the Parish Magazine too!"

"'In the last fortnight sixteen hymn books have disappeared from the church. There is no need for public scandal so if Mr. James Bagshaw, Junior, of 113 Lower Cheltenhan Place, will call upon the Churchwardens, all will be arranged.'

"That's the son of old Bagshaw, of the bank," cried Pomeroy, "What can they have been dreaming of?

"'The Vicar (the Rev. Ffolliott-Sharp, B.A.) would take this opportunity to beg the younger Miss Ormerod to desisist from her present tactics. Delicacy forbids the Vicar from saying what those tactics are. It is not necessary for a young lady to attend every service, and to push herself into the front pew, which is already owned (though not paid for) by the Dawson-Braggs family. The

Vicar has asked us to send marked copies of this paragraph to Mrs. Deknar, Miss Featherstone, and Miss Poppy Crewe.'"

Pomeroy wiped his forehead. "This is pretty awful!" said he. Then:

"'Some of these Sundays Major Wilson's false teeth will drop into the collecting bag. Let him either get a new set, or else take off that smile when he walks round with the bag. With lips firmly compressed there is no reason why the present set may not last for years.'

"That's where the answer comes in," said Pomeroy, glancing at the open letter upon his table. "I expect he'll be round with a stick presently. What's this?

"'We don't know if Miss Cissy Dufour and Captain Copperley are secretly married or not. If not, they should be. He could then enter Laburnum Villa instead of wearing out the garden gate by leaning on it!'

"Good heavens, listen to this one! 'Mr. Malceby, the grocer, is back from Hythe. But why the bag of sand among his luggage? Surely sugar gives a sufficient profit at its present price. As we are on the subject, we cannot but remark upon the increased water rate paid last quarter by the Silverside Dairy Company. What do they do with all this water? The public has a right to know.'

"Good Lord, listen to this! 'It is very wrong to say that our popular member, Sir James Tender, was drunk at the garden party of the Mayor. It is true that he tripped over his own leg when he tried to dance the tango, but that can fairly be attributed to his own obvious physical disabilities. As a matter of fact, several guests who only drank one glass of the Mayor's champagne (natural 1928) were very ill in consequence, so that it is most unfair to put so uncharitable an interpretation upon our member's *faux pas*.'

"That's worth a thousand pounds in any Court," groaned Porneroy. "My dear, Rothschild couldn't stand the actions that this paper will bring on us."

The ladies of the family had shown a regrettable inclination to laugh, but his words made them properly solemn. He continued his reading.

"'Mrs. Peddigrew has started a six-cylinder which is listed at seven hundred and fifty pounds. How she does it nobody knows. Her late husband was a little rat of a man who did odd jobs down in the City. He could not have left so much. This matter wants looking into.'

"Why, he was the vice-chairman of the Baltic," said Pomeroy. "These people are stark, staring mad. Listen to this.

"'Evensong will be at six-thirty. Yes, Mrs. Mould, at six-thirty sharp. And Mr. King will be on the left-hand seat well within view. We can count on your attendance. If you are not a pillar of the church, you are generally sneaking behind one!' Oh, Lord, here's another.

"'If Mr. Goldbury, of 7 Cheesman Place, will call at the Vicarage he will receive back the trouser-button which he put in the bag last Sunday. It is useless to the Vicar, whereas in its right place it might be most important to Mr. Goldbury!' There's no use laughing, you two. You won't laugh when you see the lawyer's letters. Listen to this.

""""Prithee why so pale, fond lover? Prithee why so pale?" The question is addressed to William Briggs, our dentist friend of Hope Street. Has the lady in pink chiffon turned you down, or is it merely that you are behind with your rent, as usual? Cheer up, William. You have our best wishes.'

"Good gracious! They grow worse and worse. Just listen to this.

"'If any motorists get into trouble, my advice to them is to see Chief Constable Walton in his private room at the Town Hall. Cheques will, of course, not be received. But surely it is far better to pay a small sum across the table in ready cash—asking for no receipt—than to have the trouble and expense of proceedings in the Court.'

"My word, we shall have some proceedings in the Court before we are through. Here is a tit-bit which will keep the lawyers busy: 'The Voyd-Merriman wedding was a most interesting affair and we wish the young couple every happiness. We say "young" out of courtesy, for it is an open secret that the bride will never see thirty-five again. The groom also is, we should say, getting rather long in the tooth. By the way, why did he start and look over his shoulder when the clergyman spoke of "any just cause or impediment"? No doubt it was perfectly harmless, but it gave rise to some ill-natured gossip. We had pleasure in attending the reception afterwards. There was a detective to guard the presents. We really think that his services could have been dispensed with, for they would never have been in danger. Major Wilson's two brass napkin rings were the pick of the bunch. There was a cheque in an envelope from the bride's father. We have heard what the exact figure was, and we quite appreciate the need for an envelope. However, it will pay for the cab to the station. It is understood that the happy couple will get as far as Margate for their honeymoon, and if the money holds out they may extend their travels to Ramsgate. Address: the Red Cow public house, near the Station.'

"Why, these are the richest people in Rotherheath," said Pomeroy, wiping his forehead.

"There is a lot more, but that is enough to settle our hash. I think we had best sell up for what we can get and clear out of the town. My gosh, those two folk must have got out of an asylum. Anyhow, my first job must be to see them. Maybe they are millionaires who can afford to pay for their little jokes."

His mission proved, however, to be fruitless. On inquiry at the address given he found that it was an empty house. The caretaker from next door knew nothing of the matter. It was clear now why the young man had waited at the gate for his parcel. What was Pomeroy to do next? Apparently he could only sit and wait for the arrival of the writs. However, it was a very different document which was handed in at his door two evenings later, It was headed

"R.S.B.Y.P,"

and ran thus:

"*A special meeting of the R.S.B.Y.P. will be held at 16 Stanmore Terrace, in the billiards-room of John Anderson, J.P., to-night at 9 p.m. The presence of Mr. James Pomeroy, printer, is urgently needed. The matter under discussion is his liability for certain scandalous statements recently printed in the Parish Magazine.*"

It may well be imagined that Mr. Pomeroy was punctual at the appointment.

"Mr. Anderson is not at home himself," said the footman, "but young Mr. Robert Anderson and his friends are receiving." There was a humorous twinkle in the footman's eyes.

The printer was shown into a small waiting-room, where two men, one a postman and the other apparently a small tradesman, were seated. He could not help observing that they were both as harassed and miserable as he was himself. They looked at him with dull, lack-lustre eyes, but were too dispirited to talk, nor did he feel sufficient energy to break the silence.. Presently one of them and then the other was called out. Finally the footman came for him, and threw wide a door.

"Mr. James Pomeroy," cried the footman.

At the end of a large music-room, which was further adorned by a billiards-table, was sitting a semicircle of young people, all very serious, and all with writing materials before them. None was above twenty-one years of age, and they were about equally divided as to sex. Among them were the two customers who had lured him to his doom. They both smiled at him most affectionately, in spite of his angry stare.

"Pray sit down, Mr. Pomeroy," said a very young man in evening dress, who acted as Chairman. "There are one or two questions which, as President of the R.S.B.Y.P., it is my duty to put to you. I believe that you have been somewhat alarmed by this incident of the Parish Magazine?"

"Of course I have," said Pomeroy, in a surly voice.

"May I ask if your sleep has been affected?"

"I have not closed my eyes since it happened."

There was a subdued murmur of applause, and several members leaned across to shake hands with Mr. Robert Anderson.

"Did it affect your future plans?"

"I had thought of leaving the town."

"Excellent! I think, fellow-members, that there is no doubt that the monthly gold medal should be awarded to Mr. Anderson and Miss Duncan for their very meritorious performance, which has been well conceived and cleverly carried out. To relieve your natural anxiety, we must tell you at once, Mr. Pomeroy, that you have been the victim of a joke."

"It's likely to be a pretty costly one," said the printer.

"Not at all. No harm has been done. No leaflets have been sent out. The letters which have reached you emanate from ourselves. We are, Mr. Pomeroy, the Rotherheath Society of Bright Young People, who endeavour to make the world a merrier and more lively place by the exercise of our wit. Upon this occasion a prize was offered for whichever member or members could most effectually put the wind up some resident in this suburb. There have been several candidates, but on the whole the prize must be awarded as already said."

"But—but—it's unjustifiable!" stammered Pomeroy.

"Entirely," said the Chairman, cheerfully. "I think that all our proceedings may come under that head. On the other hand, we remind our victims that they have unselfishly sacrificed themselves for the general hilarity of the community. A special silver medal, which I will now affix to your coat, will be your souvenir of the occasion."

"And I'll speak to my father when he comes back," said Anderson. "What I mean is, there is printing and what not to be done for the firm."

"And my father really edits the Parish Magazine. That's what put it into our heads," said Miss Duncan. "Maybe we can get you the printing after all."

"And there is whisky-and-soda on the sideboard, and a good cigar," said the President.

So Mr. Pomeroy eventually went out into the night, thinking that after all youth will be served, and it would be a dull world without it.

*The End*

# THE LOVE AFFAIR OF GEORGE VINCENT PARKER

By

· Sir Arthur Conan Doyle

The Strand Magazine, 1901

The cases dealt with in this series of studies of criminal psychology are taken from the actual history of crime, though occasionally names have been changed where their retention might cause pain to surviving relatives.

# THE LOVE AFFAIR OF GEORGE VINCENT PARKER

THE student of criminal annals will find upon classifying his cases that the two causes which are the most likely to incite a human being to the crime of murder are the lust of money and the black resentment of a disappointed love. Of these the latter are both rarer and more interesting, for they are subtler in their inception and deeper in their psychology. The mind can find no possible sympathy with the brutal greed and selfishness which weighs a purse against a life; but there is something more spiritual in the case of the man who is driven by jealousy and misery to a temporary madness of violence. To use the language of science it is the passionate as distinguished from the instinctive criminal type. The two classes of crime may be punished by the same severity, but we feel that they are not equally sordid, and that none of us is capable of saying how he might act if his affections and his self-respect were suddenly and cruelly outraged. Even when we indorse the verdict it is still possible to feel some shred of pity for the criminal. His offence has not been the result of a self-interested and cold-blooded plotting, but it has been the consequence—however monstrous and disproportionate—of a cause for which others were responsible. As an example of such a crime I would recite the circumstances connected with George Vincent Parker, making some alteration in the names of persons and of places wherever there is a possibility that pain might be inflicted by their disclosure.

Nearly forty years ago there lived in one of our Midland cities a certain Mr. Parker, who did a considerable business as a commission agent. He was an excellent man of affairs, and during those progressive years which intervened between the Crimean and the American wars his fortune increased rapidly.

He built himself a villa in a pleasant suburb outside the town, and being blessed with a charming and sympathetic wife there was every prospect that the evening of his days would be spent in happiness. The only trouble which he had to contend with was his inability to understand the character of his only son, or to determine what plans he should make for his future.

George Vincent Parker, the young man in question, was of a type which continually recurs and which verges always upon the tragic. By some trick of atavism he had no love for the great city and its roaring life, none for the weary round of business, and no ambition to share the rewards which successful business brings. He had no sympathy with his father's works or his father's ways, and the life of the office was hateful to him. This aversion to work could not, however, be ascribed to viciousness or indolence. It was innate and constitutional. In other directions his mind was alert and receptive. He loved music and showed a remarkable aptitude for it. He was an excellent linguist and had some taste in painting. In a word, he was a man of artistic temperament, with all the failings of nerve and of character which that temperament implies. In London he would have met hundreds of the same type, and would have found a congenial occupation in making small incursions into literature and dabbling in criticism. Among the cotton-brokers of the Midlands his position was at that time an isolated one, and his father could only shake his head and pronounce him to be quite unfit to carry on the family business. He was gentle in his disposition, reserved with strangers, but very popular among his few friends. Once or twice it had been remarked that he was capable of considerable bursts of passion when he thought himself ill-used.

This is a type of man for whom the practical workers of the world have no affection, but it is one which invariably appeals to the feminine nature. There is a certain helplessness about it and a naïve appeal for sympathy to which a woman's heart readily responds— and it is the strongest, most vigorous woman who is the first to answer the appeal.

We do not know what other consolers this quiet dilettante may have found, but the details of one such connection have come down to us. It was at a musical evening at the house of a local doctor that he first met Miss Mary Groves. The doctor was her uncle, and she had come to town to visit him, but her life was spent in attendance upon her grandfather, who was a very virile old gentleman, whose eighty years did not prevent him from fulfilling all the duties of a country gentleman, including those of the magisterial bench.

After the quiet of a secluded manor-house the girl in the first flush of her youth and her beauty enjoyed the life of the town, and seems to have been particularly attracted by this refined young musician, whose appearance and manners suggested that touch of romance for which a young girl craves. He on his side was drawn to her by her country freshness and by the sympathy which she showed for him. Before she returned to the Manor-house friendship had grown into love and the pair were engaged.

But the engagement was not looked upon with much favour by either of the families concerned. Old Parker had died, and his widow was left with sufficient means to live in comfort, but it became more imperative than ever that some profession should be found for the son. His invincible repugnance to business still stood in the way. On the other hand the young lady came of a good stock, and her relations, headed by the old country squire, objected to her marriage with a penniless young man of curious tastes and character. So for four years the engagement dragged along, during which the lovers corresponded continually, but seldom met. At the end of that time he was twenty-five and she was twenty-three, but the prospect of their union seemed as remote as ever. At last the prayers of her relatives overcame her constancy, and she took steps to break the tie which held them together. This she endeavoured to do by a change in the tone of her letters, and by ominous passages to prepare him for the coming blow.

On August 12th, 18?? she wrote that she had met a clergyman who was the most delightful man she had ever seen in her life. 'He has been staying with us, ' she said, 'and grandfather thought that he would just suit me, but that would not do. ' This passage, in spite of the few lukewarm words of reassurance, disturbed young Vincent Parker exceedingly. His mother testified afterwards to the extreme depression into which he was thrown, which was the less remarkable as he was a man who suffered from constitutional low spirits, and who always took the darkest view upon every subject. Another letter reached him next day which was more decided in its tone.

'I have a good deal to say to you, and it had better be said at once, ' said she. 'My grandfather has found out about our correspondence, and is wild that there should be any obstacle to the match between the clergyman and me. I want you to release me that I may have it to say that I am free. Don't take this too hardly, in pity for me. I shall not marry if I can help it. '

This second letter had an overpowering effect. His state was such that his mother had to ask a family friend to sit up with him all night. He paced up and down in an extreme state of nervous excitement, bursting constantly into tears. When he lay down his hands and feet twitched convulsively. Morphia was administered, but without effect. He refused all food. He had the utmost difficulty in answering the letter, and when he did so next day it was with the help of the friend who had stayed with him all night. His answer was reasonable and also affectionate.

'My dearest Mary, ' he said. 'Dearest you will always be to me. To say that I am not terribly cut up would be a lie, but at any rate you know that I am not the man to stand in your way. I answer nothing to your last letter except that I wish to hear from your own lips what your wishes are, and I will then accede to them. You know me too well to think that I would then give way to any unnecessary nonsense or sentimentalism. Before I leave England I wish to see you once again, and for the last time, though God knows what misery it gives me to say so. You will admit that my desire to see you is but natural. Say in your next where you will meet me. Ever, dearest Mary, your affectionate GEORGE. '

Next, day he wrote another letter in which he again implored her to give him an appointment, saying that any place between their house and Standwell, the nearest village, would do. 'I am ill and thoroughly upset, and I do not wonder that you are, ' said he. 'We shall both be happier and better in mind as well as in body after this last interview. I shall be at your appointment, coute qu'il coute. Always your affectionate GEORGE. '

There seems to have been an answer to this letter actually making an appointment, for he wrote again upon Wednesday, the 19th. 'My dear Mary, ' said he, 'I will only say here that I will arrive by the train you mention and that I hope, dear Mary, that you will not bother yourself unnecessarily about all this so far as I am concerned. For my own peace of mind I wish to see you, which I hope you won't think selfish. Du reste I only repeat what I have already said. I have but to hear from you what your wishes are and they shall be complied with. I have sufficient savoir faire not to make a bother about what cannot be helped. Don't let me be the cause of any row between you and your grandpapa. If you like to call at the inn I will not stir out until you come, but I leave this to your judgment. '

As Professor Owen would reconstruct an entire animal out of a single bone, so from this one little letter the man stands flagrantly revealed. The scraps of French, the self-conscious allusion to his own savoir faire, the florid assurances which mean nothing, they are all so many strokes in a subtle self-portrait.

Miss Groves had already repented the appointment which she had given him. There may have been some traits in this eccentric lover whom she had abandoned which recurred to her memory and warned her not to trust herself in his power. —My dear George, ' she wrote—and her letter must have crossed his last one—'I write this in the greatest haste to tell you not to come on any account. I leave here today, and can't tell when I can or shall be back. I do not wish to see you if it can possibly be avoided, and indeed there will be no chance now, so we had best end this state of suspense at once and say good-bye without seeing each other. I feel sure I could not stand the meeting. If you write once more within the next three days I shall get it, but not later than that time without its being seen, for my letters are strictly watched and even opened. Yours truly, MARY. '

About two miles upon the other side of the Manor-house, and four miles from the Bull's Head Inn, there is a thriving grammar school, the head master of which was a friend of the Groves family and had some slight acquaintance with Vincent Parker. The young man thought, therefore, that this would be the best place for him to apply for information, and he arrived at the school about half-past one. The head master was no doubt considerably astonished at the appearance of this dishevelled and brandy-smelling visitor, but he answered his questions with discretion and courtesy.

'I have called upon you, ' said Parker, 'as a friend of Miss Groves. I suppose you know that there is an engagement between us? '

'I understood that there was an engagement, and that it had been broken off, ' said the master.

'Yes, ' Parker answered. 'she has written to me to break off the engagement and declines to see me. I want to know how matters stand. '

'Anything I may know, ' said the master, 'is in confidence, and so I cannot tell you. '

'I will find it out sooner or later, ' said Parker, and then asked who the clergyman was who had been staying at the Manor-house. The master acknowledged that there had been one, but refused to give the name. Parker then asked whether Miss Groves was at the Manor-house and if any coercion was being used to her. The other answered that she was at the Manor-house and that no coercion was being used.

'Sooner or later I must see her, ' said Parker. 'I have written to release her from her engagement, but I must hear from her own lips that she gives me up. She is of age and must please herself. I know that I am not a good match, and I do not wish to stand in her way. '

The master then remarked that it was time for school, but that he should be free again at half-past four if Parker had anything more to say to him, and Parker left, promising to return. It is not known how he spent the next two hours, but he may have found some country inn in which he obtained some luncheon. At half-past four he was back at the school, and asked the master for advice as to how to act. The master suggested that his best course was to write a note to Miss Groves and to make an appointment with her for next morning.

'If you were to call at the house, perhaps Miss Groves would see you, ' said this sympathetic and most injudicious master.

'I will do so and get it off my mind, ' said Vincent Parker.

It was about five o'clock when he left the school, his manner at that time being perfectly calm and collected.

It was forty minutes later when the discarded lover arrived at the house of his sweetheart. He knocked at the door and asked for Miss. Groves. She had probably seen him as he came down the drive, for she met him at the drawing-room door as he came in, and she invited him to come with her into the garden. Her heart was in her mouth, no doubt, lest her grandfather should see him and a scene ensue. It was safer to have him in the garden than in the house. They walked out, therefore, and half an hour later they were seen chatting quietly upon one of the benches. A little afterwards the maid went out and told Miss Groves that tea was ready. She came in alone, and it is suggestive of the views taken by the grandfather that there seems to have been no question about Parker coming in also to tea. She came out again into the garden and sat for a long time with the young man, after which they seem to have set off together for a stroll down the country lanes. What passed during that walk, what recriminations upon his part, what retorts upon hers, will never now be known. They were only once seen in the course of it. At about half-past eight o'clock a labourer, coming up a long lane which led from the high road to the Manor-house, saw a man and a woman walking together. As he passed them he recognised in the dusk that the lady was Miss Groves, the granddaughter of the squire. When he looked back he saw that they had stopped and were standing face to face conversing.

A very short time after this Reuben Conway, a workman, was passing down this lane when he heard a low sound of moaning. He stood listening, and in the silence of the country evening he became aware that this ominous sound was drawing nearer to him. A wall flanked one side of the lane, and as he stared about him his eye caught something moving slowly down the black shadow at the side. For a moment it must have seemed to him to be some wounded animal, but as he approached it he saw to his astonishment that it was a woman who was slowly stumbling along, guiding and supporting herself by her hand against the wall. With a cry of horror he found himself looking into the face of Miss Groves, glimmering white through the darkness.

'Take me home! ' she whispered. 'Take me home! The gentleman down there has been murdering me. '

The horrified labourer put his arms round her, and carried her for about twenty yards towards home.

'Can you see anyone down the lane? ' she asked, when he stopped for breath.

He looked, and through the dark tunnel of trees he saw a black figure moving slowly behind them. The labourer waited, still propping up the girl's head, until young Parker overtook them.

'Who has been murdering Miss Groves? ' asked Reuben Conway.

'I have stabbed her, ' said Parker, with the utmost coolness.

'Well, then, you had best help me to carry her home, ' said the labourer. So down the dark lane moved that singular procession: the rustic and the lover, with the body of the dying girl between them.

'Poor Mary! ' Parker muttered. 'Poor Mary! You should not have proved false to me! '

When they got as far as the lodge-gate Parker suggested that Reuben Conway should run and get something which might stanch the bleeding. He went, leaving these tragic lovers together for the last time. When he returned he found Parker holding something to her throat.

'Is she living? ' he asked.

'She is, ' said Parker.

'Oh, take me home! ' wailed the poor girl. A little farther upon their dolorous journey they met two farmers, who helped them.

'Who has done this? ' asked one of them.

'He knows and I know, ' said Parker, gloomily. 'I am the man who has done this, and I shall be hanged for it. I have done it, and there is no question about that at all. '

These replies never seem to have brought insult or invective upon his head, for everyone appears to have been silenced by the overwhelming tragedy of the situation.

'I am dying! ' gasped poor Mary, and they were the last words which she ever said. Inside the hall-gates they met the poor old squire running wildly up on some vague rumour of a disaster. The bearers stopped as they saw the white hair gleaming through the darkness.

'What is amiss? ' he cried.

Parker said, calmly, 'It is your grand-daughter Mary murdered. '

'Who did it? ' shrieked the old man.

'I did it. '

'Who are you? ' he cried.

'My name is Vincent Parker. '

'Why did you do it? '

'She has deceived me, and the woman who deceives me must die. '

The calm concentration of his manner seems to have silenced all reproaches.

'I told her I would kill her, ' said he, as they all entered the house together. 'She knew my temper. '

The body was carried into the kitchen and laid upon the table. In the meantime Parker had followed the bewildered and heart-broken old man into the drawing-room, and holding out a handful of things, including his watch and some money, he asked him if he would take care of them. The squire angrily refused. He then took two bundles of her letters out of his pocket—all that was left of their miserable love story.

'Will you take care of these? ' said he. 'You may read them, burn them, do what you like with them. I don't wish them to be brought into court. '

The grandfather took the letters and they were duly burned.

And now the doctor and the policeman, the twin attendants upon violence, came hurrying down the avenue. Poor Mary was dead upon the kitchen table, with three great wounds upon her throat. How, with a severed carotid, she could have come so far or lived so long is one of the marvels of the case. As to the policeman, he had no trouble in looking for his prisoner. As he entered the room Parker walked towards him and said that he wished to give himself up for murdering a young lady. When asked if he were aware of the nature of the charge he said, 'Yes, quite so, and I will go with you quietly, only let me see her first. '

'What have you done with the knife? ' asked the policeman.

Parker produced it from his pocket, a very ordinary one with a clasp blade. It is remarkable that two other penknives were afterwards found upon him. They took him into the kitchen and he looked at his victim.

'I am far happier now that I have done it than before, and I hope that she is. ' said he.

This is the record of the murder of Mary Groves by Vincent Parker, a crime characterized by all that inconsequence and grim artlessness which distinguish fact from fiction. In fiction we make people say and do what we should conceive them to be likely to say or do, but in fact they say and do what no one would ever conceive to be likely. That those letters should be a prelude to a murder, or that after a murder the criminal should endeavour to stanch the wounds of his victim, or hold such a conversation as that described with the old squire, is what no human invention would hazard. One finds it very difficult on reading all the letters and weighing the facts to suppose that Vincent Parker came out that day with the preformed intention of killing his former sweetheart. But whether the dreadful idea was always there, or whether it came in some mad flash of passion provoked by their conversation, is what we shall never know. It is certain that she could not have seen anything dangerous in him up to the very instant of the crime, or she would certainly have appealed to the labourer who passed them in the lane.

The case, which excited the utmost interest through the length and breadth of England, was tried before Baron Martin at the next assizes. There was no need to prove the guilt of the prisoner, since he openly gloried in it, but the whole question turned upon his sanity, and led to some curious complications which have caused the whole law upon the point to be reformed. His relations were called to show that madness was rampant in the family, and that out of ten cousins five were insane. His mother appeared in the witness-box contending with dreadful vehemence that her son was mad, and that her own marriage had been objected to on the ground of the madness latent in her blood. All the witnesses agreed that the prisoner was not an ill-tempered man, but sensitive, gentle, and accomplished, with a tendency to melancholy. The prison chaplain affirmed that he had held conversations with Parker, and that his moral perception seemed to be so entirely wanting that he hardly knew right from wrong. Two specialists in lunacy examined him, and said that they were of opinion that he was of unsound mind. The opinion was based upon the fact that the prisoner declared that he could not see that he had done any wrong.

'Miss Groves was promised to me, ' said he, 'and therefore she was mine. I could do what I liked with her. Nothing short of a miracle will alter my convictions. '

The doctor attempted to argue with him. 'Suppose anyone took a picture from you, what steps would you take to recover it? ' he asked.

'I should demand restitution, ' said he 'if not, I should take the thief's life without compunction. '

The doctor pointed out that the law was there to be appealed to, but Parker answered that he had been born into the world without being consulted, and therefore he recognised the right of no man to judge him. The doctor's conclusion was that his moral sense was more vitiated than any case that he had seen. That this constitutes madness would, however, be a dangerous doctrine to urge, since it means that if a man were only wicked enough he would be screened from the punishment of his wickedness.

Baron Martin summed up in a common-sense manner. He declared that the world was full of eccentric people, and that to grant them all the immunity of madness would be a public danger. To be mad within the meaning of the law a criminal should be in such a state as not to know that he has committed crime or incurred punishment. Now, it was clear that Parker did know this, since he had talked of being hanged. The Baron accordingly accepted the jury's finding of 'Guilty, ' and sentenced the prisoner to death.

There the matter might very well have ended were it not for Baron Martin's conscientious scruples. His own ruling had been admirable, but the testimony of the mad doctors weighed heavily upon him, and his conscience was uneasy at the mere possibility that a man who was really not answerable for his actions should lose his life through his decision. It is probable that the thought kept him awake that night, for next morning he wrote to the Secretary of State, and told him that he shrank from the decision of such a case.

The Secretary of State, having carefully read the evidence and the judge's remarks, was about to confirm the decision of the latter, when, upon the very eve of the execution, there came a report from the gaol visitors—perfectly untrained observers—that Parker was showing undoubted signs of madness. This being so the Secretary of State had no choice but to postpone the execution, and to appoint a commission of four eminent alienists to report upon the condition of the prisoner. These four reported unanimously that he was perfectly sane. It is an unwritten law, however, that a prisoner once reprieved is never executed, so Vincent Parker's sentence was commuted to penal servitude for life—a decision which satisfied, upon the whole, the conscience of the public.

*The End*

Lightning Source UK Ltd.
Milton Keynes UK
UKHW011217250422
402020UK00001B/304